Harriet's
MONSTER
Diary

Property of Harriet the Monster.

For Reya, Charlie,
Arlo, Aurelia, and Reuben
—R.M.

For Mom, Dad, Joe,
Judy, Paul, and James.
—S.E.A.

Copyright © 2019 by Raun Melmed and S. E. Abramson
Illustrations Copyright © 2019 by Arief Kriembonga
All rights reserved.

Published by Familius LLC, www.familius.com

Familius books are available at special discounts for bulk purchases, whether for
sales promotions or for family or corporate use. For more information, contact
Familius Sales at 559-876-2170 or email orders@familius.com.

Reproduction of this book in any manner, in whole or in part,
without written permission of the publisher is prohibited.

Library of Congress Cataloging-in-Publication Data
2018966234   ISBN 9781641701273

10 9 8 7 6 5 4 3 2 1

Cover and book design by David Miles
Edited by Caroline Bliss Larsen and Peg Sandkam

First Edition

AN **ST₄** **MINDFULNESS BOOK FOR KIDS**

Harriet's MONSTER Diary

Awfully Anxious

(But I Squish It, Big Time)

by Dr. Raun Melmed

with S. E. Abramson & Arief Kriembonga, Illustrator

FAMILIUS

A Note About ST₄

As a developmental pediatrician, I see children every day with problems such as anxiety, poor self-esteem, ADHD (attention-deficit/hyperactivity disorder), and even screen addiction. If only these children had a set of tools available to help them address these issues! From the literature and my own clinical experience, the Stop, Take Time to Think (ST₄) Series was born. Using this technique, children can learn to recognize the incredible strength they have within them—regardless of any special needs.

Imagine the sense of accomplishment that comes when children realize that they have the power to take charge of their own bodies and minds! Children can take a few moments before responding to stressful situations or acting impulsively. They can become attentive, aware, appropriate, and, in short, mindful.

The heroes, the tools, and the scenarios in this series are all designed to build self-awareness and self-esteem. Readers can watch the characters grow and learn to be present in the moment. Consequently, the characters see improved behavior, gain more friends, and build happier families—which are the goals for the children reading this series, as well!

Of course, these tools are only intended to be a part of an overall treatment program, but empowering children and their families to take charge remains key.

Good luck!

Dr. Raun Melmed

Contents

CHAPTER 1:

The Awful, Awful Project

Some days start out pretty good.

First of all,
Bobbe made
breakfast
for me.

Bobbe is my grandmother, and she makes the best breakfast. I had strawberry monsterade and a boo-berry muffin.

I ate it all and still made it to the bus on time. And the weather was perfect—cloudy, but not rainy. Bobbe let me wear my rain boots anyway, because I love my rain boots, and Bobbe loves me.

At school, we studied Shakeshield poems during Meanglish. Mrs. Grimm let me work with my friends Marvin Monster and Timmy Tentacle. We're on the garbageball team together. Mrs. Grimm was keeping her eye on us to make sure we stayed on track. I guess we have a reputation!

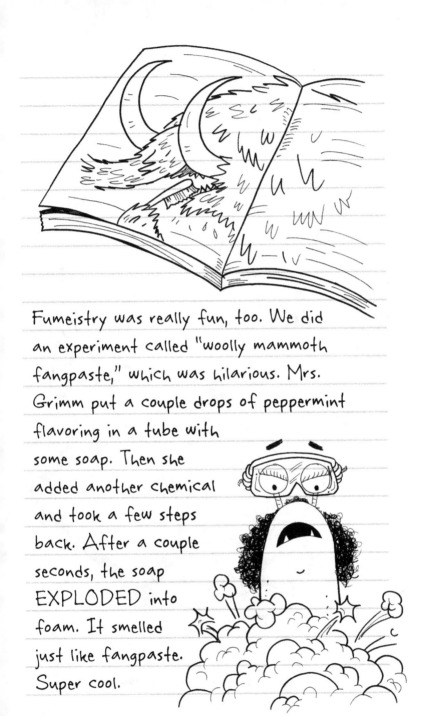

Fumeistry was really fun, too. We did an experiment called "woolly mammoth fangpaste," which was hilarious. Mrs. Grimm put a couple drops of peppermint flavoring in a tube with some soap. Then she added another chemical and took a few steps back. After a couple seconds, the soap EXPLODED into foam. It smelled just like fangpaste. Super cool.

Histroary was fine. Lunch was fine.
Recess was fine. And math was fine.

Then we had monsterology.

Usually I like monsterology. It's one of my favorites. I like learning about plants and animals and nature. That's WAY more interesting than histroary or Meanglish.

I want to be a monsterologist when I grow up. I don't know what kind of monsterologist I want to be—maybe a doctor or a scientist. It sounds so cool in my head: Dr. Ari Hairstein. Well, I guess it would be Dr. Harriet Hairstein, but either way I'd be a doctor.

11

Mrs. Grimm announced that each of us would be doing a report on an animal. The report is due on Friday, she said.

That wasn't so bad. It's only Tuesday, so it'll be nice to have a couple days to work on it.

But then she said, "And you'll read your report in front of the whole class."

I started breathing REALLY fast. I could feel my heart pounding. And my stomach didn't feel that great, either.

I can't believe it. I don't want to stand up in front of everyone and give a report! They're all going to stare at me—or worse, LAUGH at me! I hate doing speeches in class. They make my stomach hurt.

Some days start out pretty good, but they don't always stay that way.

CHAPTER 2:

Manglemane Lions

Mrs. Grimm handed out a list of animals for us to choose from and gave us a couple minutes to think about it.

She said that Timmy would get to pick first, because he's been doing monstrously well lately. He's earned THREE golden spike stickers this week!

GOLDEN SPIKE STICKER	
Timmy	◺◺◺
Marvin	◺
Harriet	◺
Penelope	◺◺
Lily	◺◺
Nate	◺◺◺
Kevin	◺

I used to think Timmy wasn't very nice. He spent a lot of time watching videos or playing games on his zaplet. I thought maybe he didn't like any of us.

But Marvin told me that Timmy wasn't so bad, so one day I struck up a conversation with him on the bus. He was actually really nice! We talked about my favorite TV show, SUPER SCARERS. Ever since then, we've been friends.

Timmy decided he was going to do his report on the kraken. Some kids in our class groaned, disappointed that Timmy chose it before they could. I don't blame them—the kraken is pretty cool. It's a giant squid that lives deep in the ocean.

Marvin picked the triple-tailed monkey. "It reminds me of my older sister, Molly," he whispered to me. I giggled.

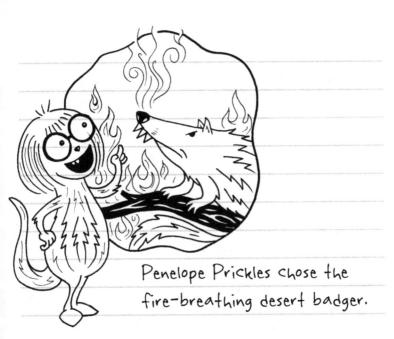

Penelope Prickles chose the
fire-breathing desert badger.

Then it was my turn to pick. Everyone was
looking at me and I felt my stomach go all
funny, but Mrs. Grimm was waiting.

I opened my mouth and tried to talk, but the words didn't want to come out.

"Ari?"

I swallowed, then coughed, then finally made myself say, "I'll take the manglemane lion, please."

My voice came out all squeaky. I hate
when it does that. I'll bet anything that
when I try to give my report, nothing
comes out but squeaks. And everyone will
laugh at me and call me a scaredy-pants.

TIMMY TENTACLE	KRAKEN
MARVIN MONSTER	TRIPLE-TAILED MONKEY
PENELOPE PRICKLES	FIRE-BREATHING DESERT BADGER
ARI HAIRSTEIN	MANGLEMANE LION

But Mrs. Grimm only nodded
and wrote my name on the board:
ARI HAIRSTEIN. And next to it:
MANGLEMANE LION.

I do love manglemane lions. They're my
favorite animal. They live in the savannas
of Scarica, on the other side of the
ocean, and are ferocious hunters that
eat grizelles and war-hogs and all kinds
of animals. They live in really big families
called prides. The male manglemane lions
have long, scruffy golden manes around
their whole faces, and their manes are
almost always a snarly mess. The females
have manes, too, but they're more like
unicorn manes, going all the way down
their backs instead.

I love manglemane lions, but that doesn't mean I want to stand up in front of everyone and talk about them. That sounds absolutely terrible.

CHAPTER 3:

My Homework Is Haunting Me

I always get home from school earlier than Mom and Dad get home from work (except on the days I have garbageball practice). They both work a lot. I get to see them later in the evening and on the weekends, but I spend lots of time with my Bobbe.

Like usual, I came home and Bobbe had a tasty snack waiting for me—monster crackers, a glass of pink monsterade, and a sour apple. My stomach still felt really weird, and I didn't want to eat anything. But I also didn't want to worry Bobbe, so I ate anyway. I was surprised that it actually helped.

Bobbe asked me how my day was. I told her about the report. I didn't SAY I was nervous—but I think she knew. Bobbe ALWAYS knows. She kept raising her eyebrows at me.

I went to my room to start on my homework. None of my assignments were that hard, but I kept getting distracted thinking about the manglemane lion report.

A session of Number Munchers on my zaplet? No problem. But the second I put my zaplet away, there was the assignment on top of my homework pile.

I put it into my monsterology folder and took out my Meanglish work instead.

We had to write a short essay about Charles Strickens. That was easy enough, but the second I finished, there was my monsterology folder again. I couldn't even SEE the assignment sheet, but just remembering it was bad enough.

I probably should have worked on the report, but my stomach kept feeling worse and worse. I still had a few days to work on it, I reminded myself, so I decided I would start some other time. Maybe tomorrow.

I finished the rest of my homework and went downstairs. Bobbe was nearly done making Weird Pierogis—yum—and Mom and Dad had just come home looking tired. They always tell me that they aren't REALLY tired—it's just that they both work with computers, so they stare at bright screens

for eight hours a day. But they sure LOOK tired when they get home from work.

Maybe I worry too much about them.

Dad smiled and ruffled my hair and asked me how my day was. I told him it was okay.

I didn't want to tell him about the report, but Bobbe caught my eye and raised one of her bushy eyebrows at me, so I knew I had to.

Mom asked me what my report was about. When I told her it was about manglemane lions, she said, "That's perfect! A lion project for our little lioness."

See, my name means "lion." Not Harriet— Ari.

Mom and Dad smiled at me. I didn't want to tell them how nervous I was about it. I just didn't want to bother them, because they already look tired all the time and it would just be something else to worry about.

33

I didn't want to tell them that it made me feel sick to my stomach. I didn't want to tell them that it felt like there was a manglemane lion sitting on top of my chest, squishing all the air out of my lungs.

Yeah, I was definitely stressed!

CHAPTER 4:

What If Something Really Awful Happens?

After dinner, I watched SUPER SCARERS on TV for a little while. Mom and Dad did the dishes together, and Bobbe sat in her chair knitting.

SUPER SCARERS was terrorific, like always. The evil Mr. Featherface wanted to build huge nests around the entire city of Scaretown so that nobody could escape from his Mega Ice-Ray Gun. But Dr. Amy McBrains and Captain Strongscale came up with the perfect solution, and their team of Super Scarers stopped Mr. Featherface just in time.

I bet that Dr. Amy McBrains never feels sick when SHE has to write a report.
I mean, she saves Monstearth every day.

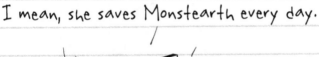

After SUPER SCARERS, it was time to get ready for bed. I scrubbed my fangs, Mom and Dad tucked me in, and Bobbe read me a story. I think I'm getting a little too old for stories, but I would never tell her that.

When Bobbe turned out the light and closed the door, I tried to go to sleep. But I couldn't stop thinking about the report.

It's not that I don't like lions or school. School is actually fun sometimes. I just don't like talking in front of everyone— I don't want to say something stupid.

What if I trip on my way up to the front of the classroom? What if my shoes aren't tied, or I trip over someone's feet or tail? I could fall and hit my face and get a nosebleed.

Or what if I accidentally say something wrong? What if I said that manglemane lions are from the tropical rainforests of South Monsteria, instead of the savannas of Scarica? Everyone would laugh and I would feel so dumb.

Or what if I do all the buttons on my shirt wrong? Or I forget to brush my hair and it looks like a mess? What if I spill my lunch all over my shirt?

WHAT IF I THREW UP? That would be AWFUL. Just the worst!

Or what if all of it happened at the same time?

I couldn't stop imagining what would happen, so I closed my eyes.

"Harriet," said Mrs. Grimm sternly, "it's your turn to give your report. Get up to the front of the class, NOW!"

I jumped up from my seat and ran to the front. I tripped over Timmy's tentacle, then over Penelope's tail, then over Marvin's shoe. My face hit the ground, and when I got up my nose was bleeding. It just kept getting worse, too—I looked down and there were food stains ALL OVER my clothes.

Trembling, I stood before the class and
opened my mouth to give my report—
but all that came out was squeaks.
Everybody laughed and pointed at me.

The door of the classroom burst open
and a whole pride of manglemane lions
pounced inside. They circled around
me and told me how stupid I was. My
stomach hurt and everyone was laughing
and pointing. The lions circled faster and
faster, and the room spun around and I
could hardly breathe—

—but then I woke up in my bed, crying.

Just because it was a dream
doesn't mean that it didn't make me
feel absolutely awful.

CHAPTER 5:

The Furmometer Is Broken, So I Try to Fix It

My stomach was hurting. I looked at the clock—it was half past midnight. I climbed out of bed and went downstairs.

Mom and Dad were sitting on the couch.
The TV was on, but they were both
asleep. I tapped Mom on the hand and
told her that my stomach was hurting.
Getting up from the couch and entering
the kitchen, she sleepily took
the furmometer out
of the medicine
cabinet and put
a little plastic
cover on the end.
We watched the
temperature on
the furmometer
go up—and then
it stopped.

My temperature was normal. That couldn't POSSIBLY be right.

"But I'm sick," I told Mom.

"Well, if you have a fever in the morning, I won't make you go to school." Mom yawned. "Come on, back to bed with you."

She took me upstairs and tucked me back into bed and kissed me on the forehead.

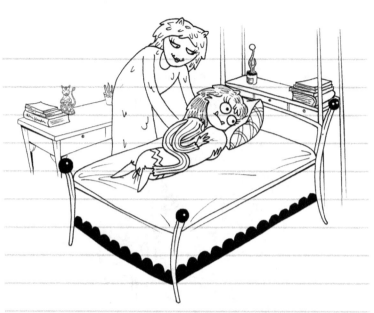

"Sorry you don't feel so good," she told me.
"I hope you sleep okay." I told her I would
try. And I did try—but I woke up again,
around four in the morning. My stomach
still hurt, but I had a great idea.

Since the furmometer said I wasn't sick, it had to be broken. I KNOW I'm sick.

I tiptoed downstairs, slipped the furmometer out of the cupboard again and turned on the hot-water tap at the sink. I waited until the water was steaming hot, then stuck the furmometer under the hot water.

The temperature went up, and up, and up. It would definitely say I had a fever now.

I turned around to go upstairs and show
Mom and Dad, but Bobbe came in.
Caught in the act! (I forgot how early
she gets up—she says early morning is the
best time to make bread.)

"And what are you doing up so early,
young lady?"

I felt silly for forgetting about Bobbe getting up so early, but I wasn't about to lie to her.

And I wouldn't have been lying to Mom and Dad, either! I really was sick, but the furmometer was broken!

I didn't think it was that funny, but for some reason when I told Bobbe the truth, she thought it was hilarious. She sat down at the table and laughed for nearly a whole minute. Then she took the furmometer and said that if I wasn't really running a fever, I had to go to school.

She did agree not to tell Mom and Dad, though. They would probably think I was trying to tell a lie, and I wasn't lying. Really.

The FURMOMETER was lying.
I KNOW I'm sick. There's got to be
something wrong with me if my stomach
is hurting and it's hard to breathe and
my hands get shaky when I think about
my report.

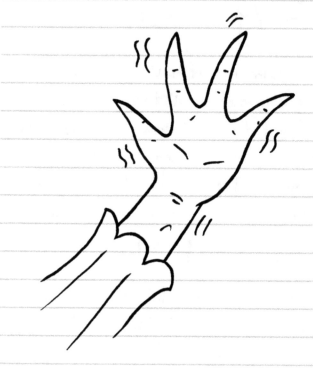

But I HAVE to think about it! If I don't do my report, I'll get a zero, and then Mom and Dad and Bobbe would be really disappointed in me.

It's only Wednesday, but I have to give my report on Friday. I really hope I get sick on Friday.

CHAPTER 6:

Bobbe Tells Me
A Story

I had to write my report sooner or later.
I came home from school on Wednesday,
did all of my other homework, and worked
on the report.

Writing it wasn't
so bad, as long
as I pretended I
was only writing a
paper instead of a report

that I would have to read in front of
everybody. And I do have this neat
book about manglemane lions.

Manglemane lions live in groups called
prides. It's usually one or two male lions,
a bunch of lionesses, and lots of cubs.
The lionesses are the hunters. They find
and catch the food, and they protect
the cubs and the male lions.

Lionesses are brave. They protect their
families and they go hunting for food.

In my family, Mom and Dad both work
and Bobbe cooks. They protect me and
they bring me food, just like the lionesses.
But I don't DO anything. I just worry
about things.

I looked at the plush manglemane lioness sitting on the shelf next to my bed. Her name is Leona and I've had her since I was really little. Bobbe gave her to me when she moved into our house. She told me that I can be a lioness.

Lions are brave. I thought about how my nickname, Ari, means "lion." But I'm not brave—I'm scared of lots of things, and I worry a lot. So, I can't be a lion.

Someone knocked at my door. It was Bobbe. I could smell something delicious coming from the kitchen—roarscht, probably. Roarscht is soup made from beets and cabbage and potatoes and, as Bobbe says, "whatever is left in your root cellar after the winter is over." We don't have a root cellar, and it's still fall, so I think it's a joke. It's definitely one of my favorite foods.

Bobbe came in and sat down on my bed.

"Ari, what's wrong?"

Bobbe always knows when I'm sad or nervous or lonely. She must have guessed something was wrong when I tried to fix the furmometer, but usually I don't know how she knows. She says it's because she's old and she's seen everything in the whole world. I don't think there's a single person who's seen EVERYTHING in the whole world, but Bobbe sure has seen a lot.

I told her that I hate talking in front of people and that I have to give my report in front of my whole class on Friday. I added that my stomach had been hurting all week.

Bobbe nodded slowly as the words tumbled free from where they had been trapped inside me. After I was done, she was quiet for a moment. Then she said,

"Well, Ari, let me tell you a story about when I was young."

I've heard a lot of stories about when Bobbe was a girl—a long time ago, far away, in another country.

We're a lot alike, which is one of the reasons why she knows me so well.

She was really tall for her age, and so am I.

She loved roarscht, and so do I.

And she, especially like me, loved monsterology. Bobbe wanted to be a nurse when she grew up, and I want to be a doctor or a scientist.

But now we have something else in common. She told me about when she came to our country for the first time. She was going to her first year of college. Back then, she didn't speak Meanglish very well—her accent was a lot thicker. She had to give a report in her first class in nursing school—and she felt sick and nervous the whole time, too!

I had no idea. It's such a relief to know that I'm not the only person who feels that way.

What helped Bobbe to not feel so nervous was breathing deeply, so she showed me how she did it.

"Breathe in through your nose, breathe out through your mouth. In, out; in, out."

But she said I should do it slowly, because it works best that way. Bobbe said that closing her eyes sometimes helped, too.

After practicing my breathing, I definitely felt better. My stomach still hurt, but I didn't feel like there were manglemane lions sitting on my chest anymore.

CHAPTER 7:

ST₄

It was Thursday, and that meant garbageball practice. We're in the off-season, so we don't have practice every single day—just once or twice a week.

I like garbageball. I'm usually pretty good at it, mostly because I'm tall and I have long arms. Marvin is good, too. Since he's shorter than most of us, he's worked really

hard on triplebounce shots. Timmy is awesome because he has a whole bunch of tentacles, so he can hold the ball in all kinds of ways.

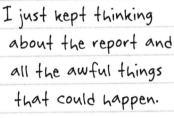

But I didn't play my best game of garbageball that day.

I just kept thinking about the report and all the awful things that could happen.

I tried to practice my deep breathing like Bobbe showed me, but I kept getting distracted. Sometimes that doesn't matter in garbageball, because the ball might just bounce off you for a good play. But sometimes if you don't focus, another team might get the ball instead.

My stomach was still hurting, and it was hard to run with that kind of pain. I tried to ignore it, and I did my deep breathing. It actually helped—at least a little!

We finished practice, and Coach Gorgon asked us to help put things away. Marvin grabbed the ball, Timmy took the sack of scrimmage jerseys, and I picked up the garbageball can. We were walking to the storage closet to put everything away when I heard Marvin ask Timmy about the report.

Timmy said he was almost done. He sounded happy about it, which just made me feel worse. My stomach was really, really hurting. I took a few deep breaths, which helped for about five seconds.

Then Marvin turned to me and asked, "What about you, Ari? How's your report going?"

I tried to answer. I really did. I breathed
and everything. But my feet stopped
walking, and my stomach was hurting
really, REALLY badly, and Marvin and
Timmy were both staring at me. Waiting
for me to say something.

I TRIED to
say something,
but instead I
burst into tears.
I HATE crying.

Coach Gorgon tried to talk to me, to calm me down, but I didn't want to talk to him. I wanted Bobbe, or my mom and dad. I was a scaredy-pants and I couldn't even give a report. Eventually Coach Gorgon gave up and howled my parents from his office phone. They were on their way anyway. If I have garbageball practice, they pick me up on their way home from work.

Marvin and Timmy sat with me outside while I waited for my parents. I don't think they knew what to do either, but then Timmy asked me if I was okay.

Part of me didn't want to say anything. I wanted Marvin and Timmy to still be my friends. And if they knew I turned into a scared little baby at just the idea of giving a stupid report, they might not like me anymore. Maybe I could tell Mom and Dad and Bobbe instead. Because they're family, so even if THEY didn't like me anymore, they're stuck with me.

But I decided to tell Marvin and Timmy about it anyway. I told them about how I hate talking in front of big groups of people and how I hate when everyone looks at me. I told them how scared I am when Mrs. Grimm asks me a question in class. I even told them how awful it would be if I tripped and had a nosebleed, or if I spilled food on my clothes, or if everyone laughed at me because I said something stupid, or if I threw up.

It makes my stomach hurt a lot !!!

Timmy was frowning by the end of it. He said he didn't understand why I was so worried, because those things might not happen. Why would I worry about something that might not happen?

But Marvin wasn't frowning. He said: "Timmy, it doesn't matter if it will happen or not. The important thing is that Ari is afraid of it happening. So, we have to help. Right?"

Timmy stopped frowning and nodded.

Then they told me about ST4.

It turns out that I knew a little about
it already. I'd seen Marvin's stickers, the
ones he'd pasted all over his folders and
binders. And I'd seen him make his hands
into a little square
in class, looking
through his hands
at Mrs. Grimm.
And I'd seen stickers
on Timmy's things, too—
his zaplet, mostly.
But I didn't
know what any
of that was for.

I learned that ST_4 stands for "Stop: Take Time To Think." They wrote it out like a fumeical formula so they would remember what it stood for. Marvin uses it to focus and pay attention. Timmy uses it to manage his time better. And Marvin explained that I could try to use it to calm down by thinking about what could happen when I give my report.

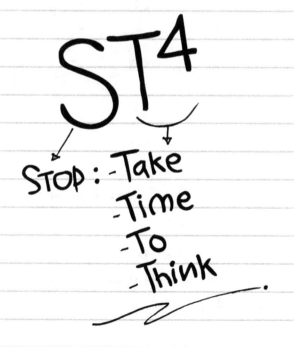

I thought that was weird. I had been trying NOT to think about the report, because it just made me feel worse. But like Timmy said—the things that I was thinking about might not happen. I was just imagining them.

So I stopped, and I took time to think. Marvin and Timmy helped talk me through the things that were scary and helped me decide what would ACTUALLY happen.

WHAT HAPPENS IF I TRIP AND GET A NOSEBLEED?

Marvin pointed out that Mrs. Grimm wouldn't make me give my report with a nosebleed. She would send me to the nurse's office first, to make sure I was okay. That was true. Mrs. Grimm is really nice, except when she's mad. And she wouldn't get mad at me for tripping, because it wouldn't be my fault.

WHAT HAPPENS IF I GET FOOD STAINS ALL OVER MY CLOTHES?

Timmy said I could either use a lot of napkins that day or I could bring an extra shirt—just in case. That made me feel a lot better.

WHAT HAPPENS IF I THROW UP?

Well, it wouldn't be like Mrs. Grimm would make me stand there and keep giving my report! She would send me to the nurse's office and get a janitor to clean everything up, and my parents or Bobbe could come get me and take me home. It would be really awful to throw up, but it wouldn't be the end of the world.

WHAT HAPPENS IF I SAY SOMETHING SILLY AND EVERYONE LAUGHS AT ME? Marvin and Timmy both had ideas about that. Marvin suggested that I go over my report really carefully, to make sure that I didn't write anything wrong in it. And Timmy said that I could practice giving my report in the mirror, so that I could make sure my voice wasn't squeaky and that I didn't say something silly. Or I could practice giving my report to Mom and Dad and Bobbe.

Today I will be giving a report on manglemane lions.

Then Marvin added in a very serious voice, "And if anyone laughs at you, Timmy and I will tell them to knock it off."

Timmy nodded firmly. "Yeah, you're our friend. We won't let anyone be mean to you."

I nearly cried again—not because I was sad, but because it was so NICE to hear that.

By the time my parents came to pick
me up, I was feeling a lot better.
Marvin and Timmy waved at me as I
left. My parents were worried because
of Coach Gorgon's phone call. But my
stomach didn't hurt so much anymore
and I had ST_4. I just needed to figure
out how to use it.

CHAPTER 8:

The Furmometer

When we got home, Mom wanted to take my temperature again because my stomach still hurt and I had been crying—and I NEVER cry. I was still hoping that I had a fever, but the furmometer said that my temperature was completely normal.

We seriously needed to get a new furmometer. Ours was definitely broken.

But the furmometer also gave me a
BRILLIANT idea.

With paper and tape, I made ST_4 signs
for myself—just like Marvin and Timmy
did. I put them on my folders and my
backpack. I taped one to the lamp by
my desk. I even stuck one to the wall
by my bed.

If I could stop and think through things
the way I had with Marvin and Timmy,
then hopefully I'd remember that things
would be okay.

I mean, KIND of okay. I still have to
give a report.

I took out
another
piece of
paper and
drew a
furmometer.
I divided it
into four sections,
and I colored them
green, yellow, orange, and red. Green
would be my Calm color—it meant I
wasn't nervous at all. Yellow meant Just
A Little Nervous, orange meant Quite
Nervous, and red meant Very Nervous.

I decided that yellow meant that I needed to use ST_4. I could maybe get over the little worries simply by thinking through the what-ifs and telling myself that they probably wouldn't happen. Because sometimes, what I THINK will happen is a whole lot worse than what actually happens.

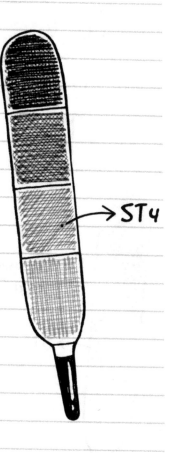

→ STY

So I wrote ST_4 next to the yellow section.

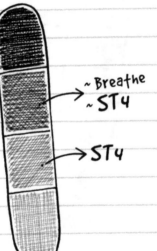

~ Breathe
~ ST4

> ST4

Orange meant that I needed to breathe. In, out. In, out. Just like Bobbe showed me. And I should keep using ST_4 as well.

So I wrote **Breathe** and ST_4 next to the orange section.

And red meant that I needed to tell a grown-up. Marvin and Timmy told me that if I'm feeling really, really sick, I should tell a grown-up. Mom and Dad and Bobbe would want to know if I'm sick, and Mrs. Grimm would help me go to the nurse's office.

And I guess Coach Gorgon would want to know why I was crying all over the garbageball can.

Even if I tell a grown-up, I still need to breathe and use ST_4. Breathing and ST_4 will only help me feel better.

So I wrote **Tell someone** and **Breathe** and ST_4 next to the red section.

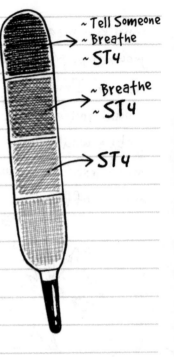

~ Tell Someone
~ Breathe
~ $ST4$

~ Breathe
~ $ST4$

→ $ST4$

When I finished making my furmometer, I took out my report and went over it really carefully, just like Marvin suggested. I went over it TWICE, just to be sure.

Then I went into the bathroom and read my report to my reflection in the mirror—twice!

My hands were shaking, so I decided that was orange on the furmometer.
I made sure to take deep breaths while I was reading my report.
In, out. Read a sentence, breathe.
Read, breathe.

And the most amazing thing happened: my hands stopped shaking.

I didn't know I could do that all by myself. It was AMAZING.

CHAPTER 9:

A Pride of Hairsteins

I knew that Mom and Dad and Bobbe were all worried about me, because Coach Gorgon had called them when I was crying, and also because I'd been feeling sick. I felt bad for making them worry. I don't like when people worry about me.

But I was thinking about it, like ST₄
says to do. Sometimes it feels like I
don't do much besides worry. But in a
pride of manglemane lions, every lion has
a job. The male lions sleep a lot, but
they're in charge. The female lions hunt
and wash the cubs and protect the pride.
And the cubs have a job, too—they're
supposed to play and grow up and learn
from their parents.

Maybe I don't really do much in my family, but Bobbe taught me how to calm myself by breathing. I like learning things. And maybe I can learn something from my parents, too.

So I went downstairs. Mom and Dad were talking quietly at the kitchen table and Bobbe was heating up leftover roarscht for dinner, but I could tell she was listening to them. I cleared my throat, and they all turned to me.

Can we go to the zoo after dinner?

I asked if we could go to the zoo after dinner.

I wanted to talk to them at the zoo because it would be easier to explain what I was thinking, about prides and families, when I could just point at the lions to make my point.

But my dad said that the zoo was probably already closed by now, because the animals go to sleep pretty early.

This was important, though—so I asked if we could go to the ice-scream place across the street from the zoo. It wouldn't be quite the same, but we would still be close. And besides, there would be ice scream.

My dad looked at my mom. My mom looked at my dad. They both looked at Bobbe. Bobbe shrugged and went back to stirring her soup. So my parents said it was fine.

Then Mom asked, "Ari, honey, are you okay?"

I was all ready to say, "Yeah, I'm fine."
But then I stopped and I thought about
it—ST4 again. Taking time to think
about things was actually really helpful.

If I were my parents and I heard me
say, "Yeah, I'm fine," I wouldn't believe
it. Not after the day I'd had.

"Um," I said. "Um, no. Not really. That's
why I want to get ice scream. And
I don't WANT to talk about it, but
I think I HAVE to talk about it." I
paused. "Also, I don't have any homework
because of the report tomorrow."

I tried to keep my voice steady, but I KNOW it wobbled.

My mom looked at my dad, and my dad looked at my mom, and then they both looked at Bobbe. I know it's a grown-up thing, when they have conversations without saying anything out loud. But it's funny to watch.

My dad asked if I was not feeling well because of the report. I wasn't ready to talk about it yet, but I was saved when Bobbe set a bowl of soup down in front of him and told him that we would talk about it at the ice-scream place.

We ate dinner and then drove to the ice-scream place across from the zoo. My dad was right—the zoo was closed. But the ice-scream place was open. My dad picked a cone of Villainous Vanilla, my mom decided on a cone with Cookies and Scream, and Bobbe chose a bowl of Ghastly Graham. And, like always, I had a bowl of Creepy Chocolate Fudge.

And so we sat in the ice-scream shop and I told them everything. I told them that I hate talking in front of people and that it makes me feel sick. I told them that sometimes my hands get shaky and that I thought I was getting sick because my stomach hurt all the time when I thought about the report. I told them about all the things I was afraid of, and I told them about crying.

But I also told
them about how
Bobbe showed me
how to breathe.
And I told them
about Marvin and
Timmy and ST₄, and how
I was going to use my paper furmometer
to help me decide how I feel.

I even told them about how I'm supposed
to be a lioness, and lionesses are brave
but I'm not. But I'm also just a kid, or
a cub, so I don't think
I know how to
be brave yet.

Saying all of this felt like throwing up, to be perfectly honest. It was hard to get the words out at first, but then I almost COULDN'T stop. I almost cried again, too. But once it was all out, once they'd heard everything—I felt so much better.

They were all quiet as I finished talking. I looked up at my dad.

He was wiping his eyes with his sleeve.

"Dad, I didn't mean to make you cry!"

"It's okay, Ari." He blew his nose into a paper napkin. "You know, being brave—like a lioness—doesn't mean NOT being afraid. Being brave means that you do what you have to do, even IF you're afraid."

"It's okay to be afraid. But it sounds to me like you're doing what you have to do," added Mom. "That's VERY brave, Ari."

"And that means you are a lioness," said Bobbe. "You're a part of our pride. Because we're proud of you."

CHAPTER 10:

I Must Deliver My Dreaded Report

Some days start out bad.

First of all, Friday morning came way too soon. Bobbe made breakfast, but I didn't want to eat because my stomach was hurting again.

ST4

Then I remembered my furmometer. I decided that right then I was at yellow, so I used ST$_4$.

I realized that if I DIDN'T eat, I would be hungry until lunchtime, on top of being nervous.

So I made myself eat. I felt better after I ate, and Bobbe was happy, too. ST$_4$ for the win!

Then I went to school. Everybody was talking about their reports, and I knew I was getting nervous again. I had the drawing of my furmometer in my pocket, so I took it out and decided I was at orange. So I closed my eyes and sat at my desk and just breathed. In, out. In, out.

I opened my eyes and saw Marvin and Timmy. They both grinned at me and gave me the thumbs-up sign. I gave them the thumbs-up back.

I was definitely not at green, but I did feel pretty good. I learned about ST_4 from Marvin and Timmy, but I came up with the furmometer all by myself.

The first class we had was histroary. I probably should have paid more attention, but histroary is sooooo boring and I ended up thinking about my report.

Suddenly, I felt really nervous. Like, orange nervous— but nearly RED. What if ST_4 and breathing and telling someone didn't work? What if Marvin and Timmy had just made the whole thing up? What if Bobbe was wrong?

And then I looked down at the floor and I saw one of the props I had decided to bring for my report peeking out from inside my backpack. And I breathed. In, out. In, out.

Bobbe WOULDN'T lie to me. I knew that. And Marvin and Timmy were really good friends. And ST_4 DID work. I'd seen it work before.

And then Mrs. Grimm announced that
we were done with histroary for the day
and we were going to start monsterology
and give our reports.

Oh boy.

THE KRAKEN

Timmy went first. He gave a neat report on the kraken. Krakens can be up to two MILES long and they live at the bottom of the ocean. We don't know a whole lot about them, but they are pretty friendly. Sometimes they wave at passing ships.

Marvin went after Timmy and talked about triple-tailed monkeys and how they use all three of their tails to do cool things like peel bananas and pick up rocks to throw at the animals that want to eat them.

Then Penelope Prickles went and gave
her report on fire-breathing desert
badgers. I mean, there's not a whole lot
to a fire-breathing desert badger, but I
learned that they only eat fire ants and
cactus juice. So that was pretty neat.

Then it was my turn.

My hands shook again and my
stomach hurt really badly. I picked
up my report and my backpack and
I went to the front of the room.

Everyone was staring at me. I closed my eyes and I breathed. In, out. In, out. Then I looked at my report.

"As you know, my name is Harriet," I read shakily. "But my parents and my grandmother and all of you call me by a nickname—Ari. It comes from the same language that my grandmother, my Bobbe, spoke when she was a little girl living in another country. 'Ari' means 'lion.' So I really like lions."

I reached down into my backpack and pulled out my first prop: Leona the lioness. Then I took out my second prop, which was my huge book on manglemane lions.

MANGLEMANE LIONS

Then I gave my report.

It was a good thing I'd practiced in the mirror, because I felt my voice getting squeaky in spots. When that happened, I paused, took a deep breath, and kept going. Mrs. Grimm didn't yell at me for taking too long, and none of my classmates laughed at me. My legs had started to shake, too.

After what felt like forever, I finally finished my report. I DID it. I grabbed Leona and my book and my backpack, gave my report to Mrs. Grimm, and FINALLY sat back down in my seat.

"Excellent work, Ari," said Mrs. Grimm. "Class, let's give Ari a round of applause."

Marvin and Timmy both turned around and gave me the thumbs-up again.

I took another deep breath and gave them the thumbs-up back.

Some days start out bad—but they can get better. With ST_4 and deep breathing, I can handle my stress and worries. I can MAKE myself feel better, all by myself.

Make Your Own ST₄ Badges

Ask an adult to help you photocopy these ST₄ badges. Color them however you'd like, cut them out, and then tape or pin them wherever you need a reminder!

A Parent's Guide to Stress and Anxiety in Children

Stress is perhaps the most common mental health challenge children experience in the twenty-first century. Stress itself is not good or bad—it simply describes the demands placed upon us to adapt to our world and to various situations. A common response to stress in both adults and children is fear. Fear is a warning signal; it is our "fight or flight" system that prepares us for action against danger. Fear can be extremely helpful, but sometimes this warning system can go into overdrive. This tendency toward heightened fear is influenced by many factors, including environment and biological predispositions. Some people are capable of coping with and responding to stressful situations; for others, more assistance might be required. It is strongly recommended that you discuss your own stress management challenges with your doctor.

We can choose how we respond to stress and deal with our fears—and that is what this book is about. Parenting a child who is susceptible to anxiety can be challenging, but fortunately there are ways you can help.

Talk about stress and fear with your child. Giving your child reassurance and a safe space to talk about feelings is a cornerstone of nurturing parenting. Let your child know that you will do your best to make the world a safer place for them, that you are there to help and comfort them.

Recognizing the signs of stress is the first step toward helping your child cope. Explain to your child that sometimes we feel grumpy, or tearful, or scared—and we don't always know why. This can happen when taking tests, speaking in front of the class, going to a new place, or meeting new people. We feel anxious or worried and sometimes feel butterflies in our tummies, our hearts beating too fast, and lots of thoughts racing through our heads.

Tell them those feelings are called "stress." Stress happens when we feel pressured to do something new or different. Feeling stressed or nervous are normal feelings, and your child can feel comfortable telling a parent when they feel that way. Teaching your child about stress and letting them know you understand can be so helpful. Knowledge is a powerful coping tool.

To help your child deal with stress and anxiety, we will need the right tools. Let's keep the tools in a **Stress Management Toolbox**.

There are two basic tools—and others that fall into these two categories—in the Stress Management Toolbox, and you can teach them to your child regardless of their age or ability. The first is for the child to describe their emotions using "I feel" statements. Whether speaking aloud or saying the words in their mind, sometimes simply saying **"I feel . . ."** can be enough to cut through the confusion and settle our worries, or at least to reduce them.

The second step is to help your child determine how to cope. That's when your child says, **"I can . . ."** In the following pages, we will discuss these tools that many kids use to cope with stress and fears.

"I Feel . . ."

Everyone experiences stress differently, whether child or adult. Help your child identify the way they feel when they are stressed. Do they make their muscles tight like a suit of armor (like what happens if someone is going to hit you in the stomach)? Do they breathe fast or hold their breath? Do they get tummy aches or even vomit? Explain that if you keep your muscles tight for a long time, they start to hurt—like a headache—and that if you breathe fast for too long you might get dizzy and feel ill.

Describing how you feel is an excellent way of getting in touch with your general emotional state. For many children, fears can be overwhelming and mystifying and can lead to a stressed state. But once children can label their worries, they can begin to get in touch with their feelings and work through their stress. It moves the ball of worry and fear from their gut and into their heads, where they can become mindful and more effectively work through their stress. So, if a child feels afraid and has a thumping heart or a tummy full of butterflies, they can know that it doesn't mean disaster will strike or that the sky will fall in. It just means that they are stressed.

Have your child answer the questions below.

1) Does your body ever feel like any of these?

- Head full of aches
- Tummy full of butterflies
- Heart full of thumps
- Hands full of sweat
- Face full of red
- Muscles full of tightness
- Nights full of scares

2) Do you often feel . . .

- afraid and worried?
- sad and tearful?
- mad and irritable?
- quiet and shy?

3) Do you often . . .

- feel scared talking in front of the class?
- forget things?
- feel picked on?
- take jokes too seriously?
- worry if people like you?

If your child experiences several of these feelings and symptoms, it may mean that they are stressed. Have them say it out loud: "I am stressed."

"I Can . . ."

Good! Now that your child has learned about the symptoms of stress, the next step is to learn what to do about them. This is the second step in stress management, the "I can . . ." step, in which parent and child determine which stress management tools work best for your child.

Teach your child three tools to manage stress: breath awareness, body awareness, and mind awareness. Here's how:

BREATH AWARENESS

Take a slow, deep breath. Count to four as you breathe in all the way, and then count to four as you slowly breathe out. Feel your body relax. Do this five times. Even doing it one time helps your body relax.

BODY AWARENESS

Tighten the muscles in your face, squeeze your eyes shut, and bite your teeth tight. Hold this for three seconds. Relax those muscles and feel the difference in your face. Do this three times. Now tighten your fists, arms, and stomach. Hold for three seconds and relax. Do this three times. Squeeze your legs together and point your toes. Hold for three seconds and relax. How does that feel?

MIND AWARENESS

After you control your breath and muscles, it is time to relax your mind. Think of a nice, calm place—maybe a beach or a forest or even your room! Imagine you are there now. Imagine what that place looks like. Try to hear what that place sounds like. Tell yourself, "I can control my body and my mind. I can calm myself down when I get upset." Say this over and over to yourself, or recite another phrase, mantra, or prayer that comforts you or helps you feel more confident.

Practice these exercises once a day at home, at school, or in the car. Bedtime works well. These tools will soon begin to help you handle stressful times. Some of these exercises might work better than others. Which do you like best? Can you think of any other exercises that might help calm your mind and body?

Harriet's "Stress Furmometer"

Another tool for the Stress Management Toolbox is the Stress Furmometer, which combines feelings ("I feel . . .") and coping ("I can . . ."). It helps children grade or color-code the intensity of their feelings and determine which coping tools to use from their Stress Management Toolbox.

Here's how to make the furmometer:

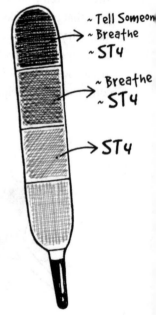

~ Tell Someone
~ Breathe
~ ST4

~ Breathe
~ ST4

→ STY

1) Draw a thermometer in the shape of a test-tube or an old-fashioned thermometer and divide it into four sections.

2) For the first or bottom section, choose a color that reminds you of feeling calm (e.g., green). Label this section **1**.

3) Now choose the color you feel when you are beginning to feel nervous (e.g., yellow). Label this section **2**.

4) The third section will be the color you feel when you are really stressed (e.g., orange). Label this section **3**.

5) The top level will be the color you feel when you are most stressed (e.g., fire-engine red!). Label this section **4**.

6) To the left of the furmometer, create a column labeled "I feel." Next to each section, write down the feelings or physical symptoms your child typically experiences for that level.

7) To the right of the furmometer, create a column labeled "I can." Next to each section, come up with coping skills appropriate to that color or level of stress. They could range from Breath Awareness for level 2 all the way to taking a shower for level 4!

Note: Creating the complete furmometer is not always easy, but the project does not have to be completed in one sitting!

Even simply identifying the level or color that represents your child's current feelings might be enough of a coping tool to head off the most major of meltdowns.

Routine and rhythms, even our innate biorhythms, are often lost at stressful times. As your child learns tools for coping—such as breath, body, and mind awareness—make sure your child maintains a routine, eats a healthy diet, and gets plenty of rest. Activities that enhance rhythmicity are very calming, activities such as playing music, swinging, biking, and—my favorite rhythmical sport—swimming. Any sport is a great stress reliever!

ST_4

Another tool that Harriet Hairstein uses to manage stress is the ST_4 process, which was introduced by Harriet's friends Marvin and Timmy in earlier books. ST_4 is designed to enhance mindfulness and self-awareness. It helps children change a situation through being mindful, thereby granting them more control over their bodies and minds. It allows children to be engaged in their own treatment process, assuring them that adults are on their side and understand the challenges they are having.

HOW TO USE ST₄

- Let your child know that they can learn to control their body and what comes out of their mouth. They can even control their thoughts! That is empowering.
- Explain what a "formula" is, like how water is H_2O and oxygen is O_2. If that concept is too abstract, just stick to the numbers and letters.
- Explain what ST_4 stands for. **S**TOP what they are doing—that's the **S**. Then they need to **TAKE TIME TO THINK**. Count the **T**s—that's four, right? One **S** and four **T**s—that's why we say **ST_4**.
- Emblazon that formula on stickers or badges.
- Place the stickers on backpacks, folders, school desks, or the bathroom mirror!
- It can be helpful to tell teachers about ST_4; they might use it in the classroom. The teacher can simply point to the sticker on the child's desk as needed.
- The formula can be kept a secret if your child prefers. Keeping it secret allows the child to develop a positive rapport with the teacher while avoiding any unnecessary humiliation by being called out publicly.

Calming Bubble Float

One last tool for your child's Stress Management Toolbox: a relaxation exercise that you can read to your child.

Let's spend a few minutes together, focusing on how you can relax your body and gain control over your thinking. Try this activity whenever you start to feel tense or worried.

Get as comfortable as you can. Good. Close your eyes and take some slow and deep breaths. Take a deep breath in and then pretend to blow out a long string of bubbles into the air. Take another deep breath in and slowly blow out another string of bubbles. Imagine the bubbles floating off into the air. See how shiny and colorful the bubbles look.

Slowly take another deep breath and continue to blow out bubbles. Feel how your body is nice and calm. Feel your muscles soften and notice how you feel more and more comfortable. You are now relaxed.

You can practice taking deep breaths and slowly breathing out bubbles at any time. This will help you deal with worries or stress. You can manage your worries with the tools in your Stress Management Toolbox. You are in charge of your body and how you feel.

Hopefully everyone is now calm and relaxed!

About the Authors and Illustrator

Dr. Raun Melmed

Raun D. Melmed, MD, FAAP, a developmental and behavioral pediatrician, is director of the Melmed Center in Scottsdale, Arizona, and cofounder and medical director of the Southwest Autism Research and Resource Center. He is the author of Autism: Early Intervention; Autism and the Extended Family; and a series of books on mindfulness for children: *Marvin's Monster Diary: ADHD Attacks!*, *Timmy's Monster Diary: Screen Time Stress*, *Harriet's Monster Diary: Awfully Anxious*, and the next in the series, *Marvin's Monster Diary 2 (+Lyssa): ADHD Emotion Explosion*.

S. E. Abramson

S. E. Abramson graduated from Brigham Young University in 2016 with a BA in English. She lives in south-central Pennsylvania with her family. *Harriet's Monster Diary* is her literary debut. She enjoys writing, video games, and anthroponomastics.

Arief Kriembonga

Arief Kriembonga graduated from Jakarta Arts Institute, Indonesia. He started his career as a children's and comic book illustrator in 2010. In addition to being an illustrator, Arief also works as a UI/UX and graphic designer. Besides art, his greatest passion is single-origin coffee. He lives with his wife and one beloved daughter in Jakarta, Indonesia.

About Familius

Welcome to a place where heart is at the center of our families, and family at the center of our homes. Where boo-boos are still kissed, cake beaters are still licked, and mistakes are still okay. Welcome to a place where books—and family—are beautiful. Familius: a book publisher dedicated to helping families be happy.

Visit Our Website: www.familius.com

Our website is a different kind of place. Get inspired, read articles, discover books, watch videos, connect with our family experts, download books and apps and audiobooks, and, along the way, discover how values and happy family life go together.

Get Bulk Discounts

If you feel a few friends and family might benefit from what you've read, let us know and we'll be happy to provide you with quantity discounts. Simply email us at specialorders@familius.com.

Website: www.familius.com
Facebook: www.facebook.com/paterfamilius
Twitter: @familiustalk, @paterfamilius1
Pinterest: www.pinterest.com/familius

FAMILIUS

The most important work you ever do will
be within the walls of your own home.

CPSIA information can be obtained
at www.ICGtesting.com
Printed in the USA
FSHW022216150319